OOEE FOUR RULING HOUSES

PLAY

OOEE FOUR RULING HOUSES

PLAY

Gift Foraine Amukoyo

Soft Grid Limited

Gift Foraine Amukoyo

Published by

Soft Grid Limited

Plot 6, Block 23, Satellite Town

Calabar, Cross River, Nigeria

+234 (0)8027676550, +234 (0)8053110637

E-mail: softgridbooks@gmail.com

softgridltd@hotmail.com

www.softgridbookslimited.com

© Gift Foraine Amukoyo

First Published in 2018

ISBN 978-978-56095-3-0

Soft Grid Books

First Printing, November 2018

Dedication

To Igoru musicians of Okpe kingdom. It would be great for such bards to resonate, chronicle activities of the society with their traditional music instruments, and compose beautiful poetic renditions.

Foreword

Gift Foraine Amukoyo's brilliantly imagined work, OOEE Four Ruling Houses, blends drama, music and verse that concoct a uniquely rewarding and entertaining piece of historical play. Set in the Niger delta region of Nigeria in the 20th century, and based upon historical events and narratives, it charts the trajectory of a royal family caught in a conundrum that ends tragically.

The play offers a significant insight into royal family dynamics and unravelling which may benefit scholars researching ancient kingdoms in this geographical area. It may also strike a chord with indigenes of the region–Okpes, Itsekiris, Ijaws and Edos, including those in the Diaspora, seeking to understand their connected histories and its complexities. Also, for those seeking to identify with the sociocultural traditions of the Okpe people, the play is thankfully a rich tapestry of folklore, songs, proverbs and poetry. OOEE Four Ruling Houses, in addition, illuminates historical narratives linking Okpe Kingdom as an emigrant community from the Benin Kingdom in Nigeria.

Intriguingly, OOEE Four Ruling Houses resonates with Shakespeare's King Lear because of its themes of loss, dispossession and, of course, a common trait of family tragedy and violent power struggle that culminates in death.

Interestingly, Amukoyo moves away from oral account in which the story has been framed over the years, deploys literary adaptation by fusing facts and fiction, and producing a speculative play that is lively with characters and dialogues aiming to articulate the fate of Egbaokpe 1 and foundation of Oreovokpe.

The Four Ruling Houses is not all about gloom and doom. There are rib-cracking scenes and dialogues providing comical relief. Moreover, there is a sense in which it portrays itself as cautionary tale, speaking to the fragility of power and the ruinous consequences of seeking, amassing and becoming drunk by it.

Dollin Holt
New Horizons Publishing Inc
London,
October 2018

Characters

Prince Igboze

Royal Guard

Oba Ahanze

Ifa Agbontaen

Olomu   -   **In-law to Prince Igboze**

Okodide

Olocho

Edokpe

Egbaokpe

Egbaokpe 1 -   **First Orodje of Ovokpe**

Egbaokpe 11 -   **Second Orodje of Ovokpe**

Olocho 1   -   **Third Orodje of Ovokpe**

Okodide 1   -   **Fourth Orodje of Ovokpe**

Izu Ovokpe -   **Wife to Egbaokpe 1**

Man

Woman

Chief Priest

Olorogun: **War Commander of Egbaokpe 1**

                             War Commander of Okodide1

Messenger

Chiefs

Otota: **Chief Adviser of Egbaokpe 1**

                        Chief Adviser of Egbaokpe 11

Isoken Tradesmen

Young Man

Warrior of Okporoko

Palace Attendant

Okporoko People

Citizens

Other Contesters

Owena

Old Woman

Nobert Johnson

Irhimvweke   -   Vweke Dancer

Supporters

Odogun Council

Prince Ogbeke Etie

Prologue

The stage lit in soft glow. It is the evening of Emobo ceremony, Egogo (ivory double bell) clings, creating a rhythmic sound to calm and lay off wild spirits from the kingdom. Prince Igboze sits upon a wooden stool. Moments later, spotlight comes upon the stage, revealing a chorus. The chorus glances at the prince, clears his throat and turn to the audience.

Chorus: *A child deceived to dance*

He must leave this land

There is nothing here for him

He is like a royal stooge

A princely stout

Without a hoarse or badge

Just look at him

He must wish he were the first

Fruit from his mother's womb

And the first strength

Of his father's loins

Even if he is the crowned prince

It still will not make any difference

Oba Ahanze sits on the throne. (Repeat)

(As the chorus berating continue in undertone, the young prince prances about the stage in melancholy. He sits on the stool again, but worry could not make him sit comfortably and he storms out of the stage in irritation.)

In the palace, enter Prince Igboze.

Prince Igboze: (Sits on the chair. He looks troubled. He stands up and turns to royal guard.) May I see the king? I urgently need to have a word with him.

Royal Guard: Either by day or night, a blue blood does not go hunting for rabbit. My prince, please forgive my intrusion. I beg to ask what troubles my prince so much that he cannot be at ease in his private courtyard and his forefather's palace.

Prince Igboze: (Impatiently) Is the king disposed? I seek his presence.

Royal Guard: There is so much urgency in your voice. I hope all is well.

Prince Igboze: In steel closed doors, the mouse still snoops around to get in. The reason I have not cut your meddling tongue with my dagger is that I cherish our childhood memories.

Royal Guard: (Grins) Yes, the rat that lives long, cracks the head of a cat. I remember how I easily wrestled you to the ground.

Prince Igboze: You could never touch my back to the red soil of my fathers' earth.

Royal Guard: (Laughs) Surely, that would have been my death. What troubles my prince, I wish to know.

Prince Igboze: The eagle's feather keeps it ever fresh; half of a canoe and the whole canoe are never equal. What do you think a chick can offer its mother hen? Look to my eyes. Do you see them smiling? Do not make jest out of my plight, not today. Check on the king, may I have a word with the Oba.

Royal Guard: As you wish, my prince.

Prince Igboze: Then grant my request, immediately.

(The royal guard bows and exits. The king appears. Two chiefs support his arms, wrists as he walks, and sits.)

Prince Igboze: (Prostrates) Oba, gha to o kpere ise.

Oba Ahanze: (Pats his back) Great cub of the home leopard.

Prince Igboze: Your highness, I wish to discuss something important with you.

Oba Ahanze: Your hammer is hard. You just want to drive the nail into the wall. Will you not share a gourd of wine with me?

Prince Igboze: (Bows) Some other day my King, if we will ever meet again.

Oba Ahanze: (Sighs) I had already sensed whatever it was, would be of great importance. The Prince does not summon the Oba from his inner chamber for mere talks. The expression on your face, and the earnestness in the royal guard's voice made me dash my hopes of having a restful nap after a meeting with my chiefs. But how can I have such leisure when the Prince is worried?

Prince Igboze: (Deeply troubled) Hands can freely roam the front of a body, but finds it most difficult to reach the back. Your highness, I want to leave the land of my forefathers to establish my own kingdom. I therefore, seek your blessings. Anoint me as an Onojie. (He Bows for the Oba's blessings.)

Oba Ahanze: (Stares stoically at the prince) The sun does not leave the place where it rises.

Prince Igboze: But the sun is not static; it covers the whole earth. It must go round to give light to other territories. It is the nature of the sun, only man assumes it does not move from a spot. The sun is a great traveller and explorer. Do not talk me out of it, my king. (He kneels before Oba Ahanze)

Oba Ahanze: Who builds a fence against a flowing River? (The king gives him coral, elephant ivory, brass, and red stones with supernatural energy.) May the gods of our land and ancestors be with and guide you to find your destiny. By the power vested on me to rule over this great kingdom, I hereby confer on you, the title of Onogie. Olokun, the god of water and prosperity shall bless your adventures as you cross any river or sea.

Prince Igboze: (Bows) Ise... (Prince Igboze packs his belongings and families to find a distant land. Light fades on them as they begin their journey.)

Chorus: *Prince Igboze, his wives and slaves,*

                 Warriors, chiefs, and priest begin their journey,

                 Passing through a mass of

Benin people who wave and

Bow goodbye to their prince of peaceful

Ordination whose departure will create a

Void in the land.

(Soft flute plays in the background. Soulful singing comes up now and again to stress conflict moments of Prince Igboze's decision.)

Chorus: *The fast progression of the Prince's convoy*

Is heard in the background,

Their walk slow down, and

Fades to a sustained urgency as

They gain ground upon a swampy Island.

(A rhythmic song play in a crescendo in a mixture of Benin and Ovokpe tunes. The sun shines downstages, revealing his new territory of Oreolomu.)

Chorus: *After days of wandering the hinterland*

The journey comes to a stop

Prince Igboze settles in Oreolomu

He finds a self-identity.

Some years later,

In the Palace of Oreolomu

The long awaited heir is born

To Prince Igboze and his wife Aghabiomo

(Drumming and singing fills the stage. Enter Queen Aghabiomo, bearing a baby bundled in white linen and a red clothe tied to his left feet. The queen walks in the company of her grand aunt and other female servants led by the kingdom's Chief Priest. Other subjects follow in a dance procession to meet Prince Igboze and his chiefs.)

It is the first male child of Prince Igboze

His daughters will have a brother

They bless him before the shrine

Prince Igboze calls upon the priest

To divine the heir's destiny

(Enter Ifa Agbontaen, a bald old man led by his white cane. He sits on palm fronds and throws four white cowries on the ground. Three assemble in one spot, while the other one spreads out differently. The priest begins his divination. He chants some Benin protective words.)

Great priest of our forbearers

The eyes of the home leopards

Tell us,

Oh, tell us seer of the world beyond

Tell us what the future holds

What has the gods predestined for the wee one?

(The Chief Priest crosses his legs, looks about the king and queen, and rests his eyes on the baby.)

Tell us oh wise one of the gods

Tell these curious people

Eager to know the destiny of

The prince

He tells them the boy's mission

As an emissary from the gods

To expand the lineage of his ancestors

With mass of land and princely sons

Ifa Agbontaen: This boy will birth four sons, and one amongst
the Princes will cause chaos.

(Dirge song plays softly)

On hearing this,

The people are not happy

Their future does not rejoice

With the royal household

They look towards the Prince for remedy

The prince ponders on how

To avert such ills to the kingdom

He must not fold his hands

And watch his kingdom

Blacken by his grandsons

The way out

Is not to crown Prince Okpe,

Prince of Oreolomu

He must go away

To another far away land

In a kingdom where his destiny

Cannot be perpetuated

The queen puts a hand on Prince Igboze

He pats her palm

She consoles him

Upon the fact that

Yet again,

The gods reject an offspring

To succeed his father's throne

The Chief Priest marks the boy on his left arm

When he comes of age

Hurdles shall be set on his path

To make him disfavor

His father's throne

And seek a new beginning

In a far away territory

But wherever he goes

The gods accompanies him

The spirits of his forefathers

Are his unseen shadows

From the day of Prince Okpe's birth

He did not know the taste

Of his mother's breast

The queen never gives Prince Okpe suckle

So that,

When the time comes

He will easily detach

From his father's homestead

From his mother's warm hut

And the kingdom that only

Gives him more of water

To drink

(Light fades slowly.)

(Light up on stage. Enter Olomu. Prince Igboze

jovially discusses with his brother-in-law from the Ejaw kingdom.)

Prince Igboze: I hope my sister treats you well.

Olomu: What can I say? I am a lucky man. You have given me the best woman any man can take to wife. It is just that the pleasures she gives on bed, is more than the delight she brings from the kitchen. I wonder about the new cravings. I find it odd.

Prince Igboze: (Laughs) We shall see the rewards of these pleasures, I think the fruit is ripening. My heir apparent to the throne.

Olomu: (Looks excited) Who thought you these matters.

Prince Igboze: Experience, experience, my friend.

(Light fades.)

Chorus: *Destiny can twine and untwine*

To fulfil the purpose of the gods

Destiny has ways to see its will

Is carried out at all costs

Five years later

Olomu and his wife

Gives birth to a son

To fulfil the vow of Prince Igboze

That he will be crowned prince of Oreolomu

It is now twenty and thirty years

After his father's ancestral voyage

Prince Okpe is enraged

When his cousin

Is made king

In order not to spill the war in his heart

Prince Okpe in rift

Packs up his belongings

With his loyalists at his heels

And he drifts further

The inland to find his feet at Agbahor

He knew his wife

OOEE FOUR RULING HOUSES

And Queen Avwudurue

Gives birth to four sons

Okodide, Olocho, Edokpe, and Egbaokpe

Without knowledge of the Priest's prophecies

Prince Okpe, profusely thanks the gods

And vows no rift

Will come amongst his princes

He nurtures them in love and togetherness

In order for his sons

To be independent off the throne

He trains them to be industrious

And great explorers

Okodide, the famous farmer

In his search for fertile land

And soil to grow more palms

Happens upon Oreovokpe

He tests the fertility of the earth

With some seedlings

The harvest is bountiful

He rejoices when he tastes

The richness of the palm fruits

(Enter Okodide, with a hoe and cutlass in hand.)

The founding father

Of Oreovokpe himself

In youthful exuberance

He leaps on stage

To share the news

Of the new land's fertility

To his brothers

(Olocho enters, obviously returning from the forest with a bush meat in hand and a trap slung over his shoulder. He shows his brothers, who gather around to praise his prowess in hunting game. Okodide shares the news to him as well. Olocho is jubilant. They exit together.)

Okodide convinces his brothers

OOEE FOUR RULING HOUSES

To migrate with him to the land of fertility

The three brothers

Will make home with Okodide

Two follows him immediately

One will join later

ACT ONE

SCENE ONE

Light shines on the four brothers on stage.

Okodide: Come, come my brothers, I have found a more fertile and spacious land.

Edokpe: I shall come with.

Egbaokpe: Wherever my brothers journey, I shall go.

(The three brothers clasp their hands together and wait upon Olocho to do likewise.)

Olocho: No, not just yet, I shall remain in Ovsoro. I will establish this land before my body, and soul will be free to take leave. Go, my dear brothers. My heart shall be with you all until I join you in Oreovokpe.

Okodide: (Holds his hand) Olocho come with. Let us journey together on this new path.

Olocho: (Shakes his head) No brother, I will stay back.

Okodide: As you wish, I will not force you, come whenever you choose, we shall be waiting.

Olocho: When do you journey?

Okodide: In the season of ohwahwa. The new region experiences high rainfall and humidity at other times of the year. The wind blows at its best. It is the best season to move so that we can build our homestead.

Olocho: Yes, it is better than the ewe season. I think that is a wise decision.

(The four brothers go in front of their ancestral shrine to pray.)

Okodide: (Sits and faces the shrine with a gourd of gin) Our great ancestors, we are here to seek your blessings. Biko, grant us the strength to establish a new kingdom. Bestow on love, wisdom, guidance, protection, patience, so that we may live together in peace and unity.

(Okodide pours gin on the floor and drinks. The gourd gets in the hands of each brother.)

Olocho: Ise… (Drinks)

Edokpe: Ise… (Drinks)

Egbaokpe: (Drinks)

(Light fades on them)

Chorus: *The first Prince*

Is weak to rule

Weariness takes over his muscles

The founding father of Oreovokpe

Does not want to be a frail warrior on the throne

He does not want the kingdom to suffer

And be vulnerable in his infirm defence

Because kingship is a symbolic spirit

And not a secular stage

Okodide will crown a strong king

Olocho and Edokpe *are at war with words*

It is unhealthy for either to become Orodje

In a crowning and anointing ceremony

Okodide crowns prince Egbaokpe, Orodje of Ovokpe-Oreovokpe.

Egbaokpe 1, the first king of the kingdom

(All exit the stage.)

ACT ONE

SCENE TWO

Close to the palace. The king comes upon a man beating his wife.

Egbaokpe 1: Hold your worthless sheath on that defenceless woman, you fool.

Man: (Bows at his feet) Your highness.

Egbaokpe 1: Guards, seize him at once. He shall spend five market days in my dungeon.

Woman: (Crawls towards the king and bows her head.) Thank you for your kindness, my lord. Please pardon my husband.

Egbaokpe 1: (Pats her back and lavisciously eyes her buttocks.) Take her to my personal chamber and prepare her for royal inspection.

Man: No. (The guards brutally hold him down.)

Woman: But, but… your highness… (She looks about in earnest indignation as the guards drag her husband off stage.)

Izu Ovokpe: (Queen comes in front of the king. Scoffs) I see you have added another to your harem of concubines.

Egbaokpe 1: (Sternly) You will have no say in this. Izu Ovokpe, your place is in the council of women to lecture and counsel them as much as you want. I hope my favourite soup is ready. Ovwo soup and boiled plantain is what I desire to eat for lunch. So say no more and do the needful. (Izu Ovokpe bows and exits)

(At the palace of Oreovokpe. The king addresses the chiefs and some subjects.)

Egbaokpe 1:   I need not remind you all, that pronouncement of the Orodje is authoritative. Therefore, no man shall question my words. My decisions are law. Ovokpe will go to war with Avwukeye.

Olorogun: (Turns to Chief Priest) Chief Priest, ears of the gods, you have heard the final decision of the king. What is our fate in this forthcoming war?

Chief Priest: Egba, the god of war does not make loud cries at Ikeresan because our community is free of any impending danger from an outsider. Oreovokpe should not make ally with warfare, or dark siege will befall the kingdom. (Closes eyes) I see something else, there will be a festival of prying masquerades, spinning canes in circle of rituals, splitting crowd with splashing sticks, in frenzy cries, the villagers will scamper for safety, bleeding from tear to tears.

Olorogun: (Bows) My Lord, I think you should reconsider your stance. Going to war is unwise. If we advance on any war, Egba will not be present to direct us on how to enforce our mercenaries and attack the enemies. The spirit will not divine the medicine to use in killing the potency of bullets, arrows and make us invisible to the enemies' swords. We will have no scabbard from the gods. My king, Egba will not defend us in this kind of battle, because this war would be a lie.

Egbaokpe 1:   Olorogun, why do you fidget? Have you become friends with the enemy?

Olorugun: (Shakes his chest) May the gods forbid.

Egbaokpe 1:   How then will the Crocodile cry in the River? Let me remind you, you are not beyond my wrath; you cannot escape my castigation if you act otherwise to this kingdom. You show disrespect by calling my decision unwise. Do not be an Okhion-Oba. It is sacrilegious and an abomination, you will not be able to bear the consequences.

Olorogun: (Bows) Whenever an animal that fought its way out of a trap, sees a stick bent in the likeness of another trap, it must take extra caution. The left hand was likely reserve to do the dirty works in the latrine; it wipes the anus better than the right would ever do. My Lord, your words will not stop me from stating the truth. I have the gods' backings to keep our people safe.

Egbaokpe 1:   (Enraged) Your utterances reel with felony. Guards, seize him at once. We shall cage his treasonable acts before it ruins us all. There shall be twenty-four hours surveillance at his house. Some guards will watch his family under the eagle's lenses.

Messenger: (Comes in and bows) My Lord, the tradesmen from Isoken has come. They wait in your outer chamber.

Chief: (To Otota) What have they come for?

Otota: (Bows to king.) My Lord, let us not tarry. Let us find out. We will address any form of unrest that rears its head in our kingdom with immediate effect.

Egbaokpe 1:   My good-natured chiefs, shall we proceed to welcome our honourable guests?

Otota: I believe we shall, your Lordship.

Chiefs: (All chiefs on one knee, place elbow on their palms and hail the king) Umogun, Umogun,

Umogun. May you live and reign longer than your forefathers. Ise.

Egbaokpe 1:   (Raises his staff of office to the chiefs) Kada.

(All the chiefs file out in their red beaded attires on white apparel and proceed to the outer chamber.)

Tradesmen: Umogun, Umogun, Umogun. May you live and reign longer than your forefathers. Ise.

Egbaokpe 1:   Kada.

Tradesman 1:   Your highness. We bring great news and good tidings from our land.

Egbaokpe 1:   Of what greatness is it? Speak of the good news. Bring great pleasures to our ears. Otota, do carry on with the affairs of the meeting.

Otota: Wo ne sutoo Umogun, Umogun, Umogun. (Clears throat and turns to the representative tradesman.) In your bond with the white men, your merchants have caused us setback in the trades market. They sell palms at lower rates not fit at all for profits. It is good your Olu has sent his emissary to broker trade peace. Ejaw and Isoken traders are now intermediaries between European supercargoes and merchants on the coast. This makes Oreovokpe run a great loss. We hardly know where we stand in the markets while you all enjoy our hospitable frontiers for commercials.

Tradesman 2:   Honestly, we are weary of this rivalry among our kingdoms. Palm oil should not cause war among us. That is why we are here to deliberate on the way forward. War is not a solution to peace; it only breeds further unrest.

(All parties go into deep discussions that are mute to the audience.)

ACT ONE

SCENE THREE

Egbaokpe 1 and Chiefs seat in a meeting. Sweaty young men run onto the stage and fall at the Orodje's feet.

Young Man: Your highness!

Otota: (Irritatingly) Have you forgotten your manners. All hail the king. Loyal subjects hail the king. You misguided sons of Ovokpe, be reminded of our great courtesy to the throne.

Young Men: (All on one knee, place elbow on their palms and hail the king) Umogun, Umogun, Umogun. May you live and reign longer than your forefathers. Ise.

Egbaokpe 1: (Raises his staff of office.) Kada.

Otota: You may speak.

Young Man: Your highness, on our way from the pond, we saw a clan at the plantation by the road. They were harvesting palms.

Egbaokpe 1: (Stands from his seat and the force makes him drop his staff of office.) What, who are those that want to desecrate the land? Did we not decree that during Edjokpa festival, no man or woman should cultivate palm. The people of Ovokpe kingdom are restricted from harvesting palm for three weeks. Do they want the deity that inhabits the most productive palm trees across our communities to withhold its blessings from us? We have few more hours to end this celebration, just this day to mark the end of our festivity, and now this. (Turns to the town crier) Go; summon the houses of Okodide, Olocho, Egbaokpe, and Edokpe. Send words to Mereje, Okwetolo, Opuraja, Elume, Adeje and other villages. Wail words of this atrocity around the kingdom that a sacrilege has been committed against the deity, which puts the kingdom's great source of revenue and livelihood at risk. (Turns to chiefs) The Edjokpa should be dressed in expensive white and red cloth from top to bottom. Get ready. We will offer the dog for sacrifice before dusk goes to final sleep. As for that rebel clan, they shall feel the weight of Egbaokpe's wrath.

(Light fades)

(The Palace. The next day-Morning. The Orodje is sitting. He accuses the palace messengers of default to his instructions. The atmosphere is intense.)

Egbaokpe 1:   (Furiously) You defy my orders.

Messenger:	(Prostrates) No my Lord, not on my life will I dare incur your wrath.
Egbaokpe 1:	Then why, have the people not carried out my instructions? (Messenger keeps mute for long.) Have you suddenly gone deaf, or your tongue is string to your jaws?
Messenger:	No, my Lord.
Egbaokpe 1:	(Impatiently) Who tends the plantations?
Messenger:	My king, the people are not happy; they will not go to the farm. The people say you mete out ill treatments to them.
Egbaokpe 1:	What guts you have. Is that the answer to my question? I see they have made you their spokesman.
Messenger:	No, my Lord. I am just lending a voice from the depth of humanity, from my human conscience, my Lord.
Egbaokpe 1:	I see now. Therefore, I am the beast without a conscience.
Messenger:	(Looks away) You unjustly force words out of my mouth, your highness.
Egbaokpe 1:	(Angrily turns his back to the audience) I shall

show off to the whole kingdom, what it is to dwell in a jungle. I am the beast right? I shall roar fire and brimstone. Whomever that dares my fury will burn, man or woman will burn.

Otota: Ariromo, your highness, be calm.

Egbaokpe 1: (Turns to messenger) Leave my presence at once. I loathe the face that ridicules orders from my throne.

Otota: My Lord, you should take things easy on your people. Caution is required on this. It is few hours after we concluded the Edjokpa festival, and you plunge the people into harsh labour. I dare say the unholy path you choose to tread will have no good outcome. He who brings a disabled person will take him home.

Egbaokpe 1: Am I unsafe in my own kingdom? I shall rule and treat my people whichever way I deem fit, nothing can stop me.

Otota: The Lion and the Elephant contest growth and size out of ignorance. The elephant has both height and strength, and that leaves the lion at a disadvantage. My Lord, I have not said you cannot do to your people what you will, but be gentle. The world has heard that we, the Ovokpe people are an Elephant, we carry ourselves with giant strides. My king, this kingly stool is thronal. Do you forget that all sons of Ovokpe are princes that you treat them like slaves?

Egbaokpe 1:   (Laughs sinisterly) They shall labour more. Now, I need entertainment. It has been long the warriors of Ovokpe tested their strength.

Otota: (Looks resignedly to the audience.)

Egbaokpe 1:   (Turns to messengers) Climb the top of coconut trees and beat Ozu-mother drum to announce my summons. I want every man, woman and child of Ovokpe community present in my palace before sundown. The contest shall begin when evening falls.

(The same day-Evening. The king nominates Okporoko and two other communities to break iron bars.)

Okporoko Warrior: (In an aside, to palace attendant) You cannot live in the river and not bring fish home. You must do something to make us victorious. Remember, it is what the hand caused that the head pays for. Do you want the downfall of your clan? Son of Okporoko, answer me.

Palace Attendant: (Sighs) Before the event, I shall secretly sew the iron bar and cover it with grease. I will help my clan. (They shake hands and exits.)

(The contest takes place in the palace. The warrior from Okporoko easily breaks the iron bar. His victory excites the crowd.)

Okporoko People: I iye! Very great...Aghwie abo (Clap hands)

Egbaokpe 1: (Stands up) For this glorious feat, Okporoko is Osia, today and forevermore.

(The people of Okporoko dance in circles and rejoice over their victory.)

Other Contesters: (Sad) Our fate will be gruesome.

Egbaokpe 1: For others that were unable to break these iron bars to prove your strength, death awaits you. (Dirge song plays softly)

Other Contesters: There has been a folly here. What man can break iron bars with bare hands? We suspect sorcery; supernatural powers must have been behind that strength. The act was immortal.

Okporoko Warrior: Ofian! Your majesty these are lies.

Other Contesters: We found out, that one of the palace attendants is of Okporoko house.

Egbaokpe 1: If you knew these, why did none of you bring it

to my notice prior the contest?

Other Contesters: We were without proof.

Egbaokpe 1:   Talks of weaklings. (Turns to guards) They are not fit to be among my army. Take them away. They shall face death sentences.

Other Contesters: (Kinfolks wail) Oh your majesty, please have mercy upon us.

                      (The palace guards shove the other contesters off stage.)

ACT ONE

SCENE FOUR

In front of the palace, people of Ovokpe, young men and women with hoes, cutlasses, and palm fronds tied around their waist assemble to protest. They cry out in agony of the hardship meted on them.

Chorus:
E, urhomu erhomę eki rhom' odę o,

Are otu akpọ,

Ọwo vbo hwihwiwi ọwa-a o,

Ẹvbe orho kpe ọmọ Oluko,

Ni da ro Ẹvbe r'ọmọ Oluko ọrhọ dua,

Ehwihwiwi ọgọrọ,

Ọgọrọ oji ghwe,

E, otele oma mę are alalọ.

(Egbaokpe 1 appears. His chiefs flank him. The maids spread a mat. He steps majestically on it, staring at the people with consternation as they murmur in disapproval and grunt out their displeasures. The people touch their body parts that hurt from labouring so hard. They murmur loudly.)

First Chief:
People of Oreovokpe, young men and women of our land, can we have some semblance? Did you

forget your manners at your doorsteps? You stand before the Orodje in his very own palace.

(The murmur builds up.)

Second Chief:	Silence, silence I say.
Citizens:	The sufferings have reached our hearts, it chokes our breath, and we cannot keep silent anymore.
Second Citizen:	Yes, such SILENCE is death, and we refuse to die in cowardly and miserable manner.
Third Citizen:	Death or justice.
Citizens:	(With thunderous shout) Justice.
First Citizen:	Today, we shall have freedom. People of Oreovokpe, today our Orodje will tell us why he treats us no less than slaves and tramples on our dignity as a people.
Citizens:	(With buoyancy) We will restore our dignity as a people.
First Citizen:	(Stands in front of the people) We have the willpower to take it back. Great people of Ovokpe kingdom, do I speak with your tongues.
Citizens:	(They shout) Yes.

First Chief:	Silence, silence, I order you by the crown to keep quiet.
Egbaokpe 1:	(Unperturbed) Do not restrain their tongues. Let them spill whatever garbage they have picked up from market dumpsites. (The king steps away from the mat.) Whoever dares my authority should step on the mat. Step onto my place and let the gods trample any fool to burn and rot.
First Citizen:	We know our boundaries. Unlike you, your highness, our most revered king who is supposed to bring succour to his people, is the harbinger of woes upon our land. The gods cannot do us such harm than you have. Who will comfort our troubles if not our gods, and to the ancestors' bosom, we submit our pains. In these turbulent times, we do not look up to the king, but to the gods.
Second Citizen:	You are the crowned king because you bore peace and strength enough to carry the affairs of our great kingdom. But today, you use your weight to crush your subjects and your peace has ceased to exist upon the face of our land and in your heart.
First Chief:	(Turns to the people) I know what you all feel in your hearts.

First Citizen:	We do not think you do. Grievous offences are being committed against the poor helpless people all over Ovokpe. No one, none of you is able to point at our harbinger of woe to steer positive change.
First Chief:	Do you think as council chiefs to the Orodje, that we are not concerned about the plight that plagues our land?
Citizens:	No, you are not; we carry the cross, alone.
Chiefs:	You are not alone in this.
First Citizen:	Palm trees are crushing our men. Our Orodje relentlessly punishes us to fall palm trees at the detriment of our lives.
Second Citizen:	Our mighty warriors have become limbless and deceased in trying to split iron bars. Dear Chiefs, do not say you feel our plight, you know not an ounce of what we bear.
First Citizen:	And our wives, who will rub ointment on our backs to sooth our aches and caress our maleness, our king cart them away to his realm of concubines. (The Chiefs bow their heads in shame of the king's act.)
Egbaokpe 1:	(Furiously) The time you waste can be utilized

to cut down more palms? Listen, all of you. It is the season of ederherhe. Whether you like it or not, four hundred barrels of oil must be ready for exportation come edebi; we must prepare for sales. Guards, gather them to the plantation. They shall toil incessantly. We should also avert the curse, which that unruly clan wants to incur from Edjokpa. We must suppress the curse at all cost. This harvest shall be fruitful.

(The guards march the people out of the palace. The Chiefs shake their heads. Light fades. Later, light shines on Owena, sewing on the floor, sitting feet away from the king.)

(Loud weaving comes from the artist' needle and thread; the royal artist weaves a red bead.)

Owena: (Clears his throat) My Lord, I beg you have mercy on our people. This act is unbecoming of our great ruler.

Egbaokpe 1:   (Calmly) Owena, the skilled artist of our time. Your placement on the high social and royal ladder in the kingdom is to display the beautiful arts of our people. You are an accomplished artist, and you have therefore earned your place in my heart and the peoples'. I would like you to stay within your limits.

Owena:	My Lord, my humble request is…

Egbaokpe 1: (Raises his hands to stop him.) Say no more. It will do you well to stay within your limits. Yours is to weave beautiful arts and not to trade words with your king. I cannot grant any of your requests. Concentrate and design not an ugly looking wrapper for me.

Owena: (Bows) Cut off my tongue if I ever speak on this matter again. And I shall chop off my fingers, if I ever create ugly arts, my Lord.

(Light fades gradually into dim light focused on the Orodje. He is in deep thoughts.)

Otota: What bothers my king?

Egbaokpe 1: I have some strange feelings. My divining spirit tells that the people have staged an evil ploy against me. However, I cannot place from which enemy camp.

Otota: My Lord, Olorugun has stayed too long in your dungeon. Who will protect you when the enemies call with their battle-axes, oil, and poisonous arrows?

Egbaokpe 1: (Resolute) No, Olorugun will rise against me.

Otota: Your highness, your own cannot rise against

you. Temper justice with mercy.

Egbaokpe 1:   (Sigh heavily) Go and hang the Egbe across the road, at the entrance of our community. The deity's medicine wrapped into a mat will keep peace and stop any form of evil from gaining entrance into our kingdom. Go, go, and let Egbe render the powers of the enemies useless.

Otota: Rọ ha otọre na. That is on ground, my king.

ACT TWO

SCENE ONE

(In the Palace. The Orodje, Olocho, and Edokpe have intense discussion.)

Edokpe: My Lord, you must handle your people with care.

Egbaokpe 1: You really think an injustice is mete on them. If my people do not work on the communal plantations, for growth and development for its future, who will? Is it I that am never to hold a cutlass in my life? I have done my piece of farming in preparation before my coronation. You do not expect me to dress up as a peasant and plough the soil. They must work. (Turns to Olocho) Should I go to Ovsoro to seek labourers, when Oreovokpe boasts of able young men and women?

Olocho: Eye se aye rhe, ihworho. Go and invite them, they are our people. Wherever there is trouble, there would be need to invite someone to help. We should cry out to invite a rescue team. My Lord, your crown veers far from humanity. You do as you please and it is not healthy to your reign. Your violation of their human right collectively wound the people's pride. Let the great rainmaker place containers to gather the water, and the flower that goes on a procession does not get missing in it.

Edokpe: (Mildly) In the first place, your installation had caused many controversies. Your Majesty, have you forgotten yester years so soon? The people had felt you were not the right prince to ascend the throne.

Egbaokpe 1: Oh, I see. Oh, I hear the feet of treason hurrying to my throne.

(Drums beat loud to announce feet running very fast.)

Messenger: (Runs in, panting) My king, the women have climbed palm trees. They strike their axes and cutlasses on the trees in order to help their sons, husbands, and betrothed. They sit upon the felled trees to rest from the hard labour.

Edokpe: (Alarmingly) Your highness, I sense grave danger. Women do not climb palm trees in our land. This is a bad omen. The palm tree is omiomo. No, your highness, this does have to stop. Women cannot eat of their own womb.

Olocho: Do you derive pleasure in seeing our people crushed by the weight of the palm trees?

Edokpe: My Lord, do not undermine your people. It is

not too late to win their love and trust again.

Egbaokpe 1:   Do the people of Oreovokpe know love? Do they really regard my throne?

Olocho: My Lord, Oreovokpe is the breast of love. That is why you are on the throne. Love has made you king. Be wise.

Egbaokpe 1:   Do you think I am foolish? Oh, I see, you talk to your king arrogantly. You forget your place. You forget, Olocho, that I am king.

Olocho: (Bows) My Lord, I am ever loyal to your throne. As a senior political leader of our beloved Ovokpe land, you have to listen to Edokpe and me...

Egbaokpe 1:   You shall be, by the gods, you shall be ever loyal to me, even if your thoughts were planning to default. Guards. (Four guards rush in and kneel in front of the king). Get every member of the immediate ruling houses that is not a descendant of Egbaokpe. Take them to the mine; they shall break iron bars from sunrise until I decree otherwise. Go now and seek them from their huts, farms and anywhere else they may be. (Light fades on them.)

ACT TWO

SCENE TWO

(Drums. Enter CITIZENS of Ovokpe. They form a round circle)

Citizen 1: Instead of our king to solve our marital issues, he takes away our troubles by coveting our wives. How long should we continue to digest this vicious circle of injustices?

Citizen 2: A leader that loses moral and his obligations to his subjects, and come to destroy the lives of his people; our god is greater than he is.

Old Woman: We shall revolt these ill treatments. The king must get a taste of his own medicines. If a medicine man goes to perform, he treats someone, and the patient dies in his presence, if he spreads his divination pellets, he does not remember to pick them up.

All: Yes we must revolt.

Citizen 1: The witch or wizard, who afflicts one, is the same person who pretends to treat us. In what is good, we find evil. There must be a revolution in Ovokpe land to unseat this tyrannical king even if it is by death.

Citizen 2: The gods ordained Egbaokpe 1 as the Orodje. He is our anointed king. An assassination on the king will be a curse upon our kingdom; such act will have serious effect on Ovokpe. Let us look for a bloodless alternative. We should rather plead to the King to change from his evil ways.

Citizen 1: Who pleads with a vindictive oracle?

Citizen 2: Then how do we intend to defeat this enraged oracle?

Citizen 1: We will try, and if we succeed, then it is the will of the gods.

Old Woman: We are tired of his brutalization. We must end his brutality; this bad rule has to end. Enough is enough.

(Sad flute plays. The people prepare their weapons.)

Chorus: *Ba Umogun osiye oghwa,*

Otu erieda irha 'obo ghwolie,

Umogun mi rhe vbo eda,

Gbe me kpe me,

Ejo, mi rhe vbo-o,

Gba nya ji me vbo,

E, ame imeba ame t' onana,

Uhu r'awa mẹrẹ zẹ,

Are ọvo ah' obọ ghwọlọ uhu,

Ọke r' uhu n'ọrhọ rhe ne o,

Gghwu s'ọmo ene kperi se?

Iti obo r'obọ 'soro,

Ghwu s'ọrana y'urhomu olele o.

Oshewere o,

 Inene o, ame rha t'ona o,

Ari ne seyi efian (Ẹvbariẹn)

The town square of Ovokpe. (The people of Ovokpe secretly dig a pit, and then cover it with sticks and mats. They place the Orodje's chair on the hole. The villagers sing the King's praises in resonating voices and drums beats. There are cheers and dancing as Royal drums break into singing.)

Citizens: Umogun, Umogun, Umogun. Wo ne sutoo…
(They hail the king as he majestically strides on the mat to take his seat. Just one more step to the seat, Egbaokpe 1 stops.)

Egbaokpe 1:   (Whispers) Otota, my body and soul do not feel right today. I have a strange feeling against my throne. My crown is threatened.

Otota: My Lord, you cannot retreat from this gathering. They organized the ceremony in your honour.

Egbaokpe 1:   (Confused) But why should they celebrate me?

Otota: (Speaks reassuringly) They celebrate their king.

(Egbaokpe 1 advances on the chair. He sits and falls into the pit. The people surround his fall with angry faces. Their weapons of vengeance poised.)

Citizens: Now let him pay for the suffering he brought upon our land and families.

(The people pour hot oil and hot water on the fallen Orodje. They throw pepper and cooking ingredients on him.)

Citizens: We have wept for too long without consolations.

Chorus: *Oh Orodje*

They strip you off the throne

Dying,

The king cries out in agony

He is bitter to what his

Disloyal subjects do to his throne

He curses Ovokpe

(Drums)

Egbaokpe 1:	(He uses his staff as advantage to climb out of the pit.)
Citizens:	(Pushes him. Egbaokpe 1 lets go of his royal staff and falls into the pit.) Haul sand on him, quickly.
Egbaokpe 1:	(In agony) For every man, woman, child that has brought this great folly upon my crown and throne, I curse you today. You will never know peace. This kingdom will raze in disunity; you shall never be able to crown an Orodje in peace. Mark this day, remember these words, for your atrocities upon your king, sons and daughters of Ovokpe kingdom will never unite under an Orodje. He shall not speak your tongue, and there shall be disunity among your generations. Strangers will rule over you. They will covet the land and benefits of Oreovokpe.

(They pour sand on him. Egbaokpe 1 continues until he breathes his last. Half of the staff unburied. The people rejoice at his death. They invade the palace and reconcile with their wives.

Light fades on the stage. Moments later, the stage comes up in fireworks effects.)

Chorus:

Oreovokpe burns.

There is bloodshed in the kingdom

Loyalists of the late king set the capital city on fire.

There is disaffection among the ruling houses.

Many flee the city and those

Whose feet are too slow, are victims.

Oh Ediọn, please protect us,

The day preceding our next worship,

We shall preach around the town.

Oh Ediọn, please protect us, protect us,

The day preceding our next worship,

We shall preach around the town.

Due to political unrest in Oreovokpe

Many people desert Oreovokpe

To find new settlements

For many decades

Ovokpe is without a king

The interregnum causes mockery

The affairs of Ovokpe is governed by

Ovruno of Okodide ruling house,

Ovwero of Olocho ruling house,

Evweke and Ovsakpe, of Edokpe ruling house

They dominate Ovokpe government and politics,

There is no role for the Egbaokpe ruling house

The Ovokpe people under the leadership of these elders

Restores their land,

With victory in Usapele land dispute

For Ovokpe people against the Isoken people

After the assassination of Egbaokpe 1,

Ovokpe is unable to crown another king.

It is a thing of shame

Neighbours mocks Ovokpe

For being a bell without a sound

Ovokpe people comes together to perform rituals

They seek forgiveness for their crime.

The sun gives verdict to the water

The eagle's feather does not let it fade,

The unity of Ovokpe people will lead them far.

(Drums. Light Fades.)

ACT TWO

SCENE THREE

(Ovokpe. The stage is dark.)

Male Voice: For one hundred and sixty-six years, we have been without a king. Ovokpe kingdom is a young adult without tooth in his mouth. We can neither crack nor chew kola nuts where kingdoms with kings meet.

Female Voice: I hope the gods bless us with an Orodje. For how long should we atone for our sins?

Male Voice: As long as it takes Ovokpe to completely heal, with love, peace, and unity. I believe it will be soon.

(Light Fades.)

Light comes gradually on stage in the palace. Oreovokpe crowns Egbaokpe 11 as Orodje. There is jubilation. With the accompaniment of Ukiri (short drum) Azuzu (manual fan) and Abo (clappers), Igoru traditional music plays in the background by adult men and women. A woman leads the vocalists. They majestically move their bodies to the melo-rhythmic stimulus of the drums and the vocal sections with different sounds:

Kiki kọngigi kọgọn or kiki kẹngigi kẹgẹn (for the mother ukiri)

Kikọn kikọn kikọn kikọn (for the baby ukiri)

Kẹkẹgẹn, kẹgẹn kẹgẹn kẹgẹn (for varied ukiri).

Chorus:

But the curse reigns

The British Government

Rejects the people's choice

Oh, the curse dwells

Orodje Egbaokpe 1, biko

It is years after the people of Ovokpe

Installs Egbaokpe 11 as king

They wait for the colonial government

To declare him as Orodje of Ovokpe

However, their inconsequential consent

Did not stop them from

Respecting the divinity of their ancestors

The people of Ovokpe freely regard Egbaokpe 11

They recognize him as spiritual royal father

Three years later,

British government reverses their opposition,

And duly recognize Egbaokpe 11 as king

(Light Fades.)

ACT TWO

SCENE FOUR

(In the palace. Light shines on Egbaokpe 11 and chiefs.)

Otota: Your highness, neighbouring communities extol your strides in the developmental growth of Ovokpe. The just constructed inter-village and inter-clan roads are the talk of the kingdom. In your reign, schools, maternity centres, and dispensaries are now available in the kingdom. Social equality shall thrive in our society. Nevertheless, do we just sit down and watch the Isokens contend ownership of our land? We should not put our hopes on the white man to settle this old dispute amicably. If you follow a fish as an inexperienced swimmer into the creeks, it's nobody's fault if you drown. We should be vigilant now that we harbour many Isoken people in our communities. We should take care so that they will not outrun us and take over our entire land.

(A messenger comes to announce the arrival of the white traders.)

Norbert Johnson: (Bows) I greet you my King. Our thirty horsepower craft made our voyage a splendid experience through the Benin-Ethiope River.

Egbaokpe 11:   (Nods) I am glad you had a peaceful journey.

May we know what brings you and your entourage to Oreovokpe?

Norbert Johnson: We bring you message from Her Royal Majesty. It is great to be here your highness, the bush paths were not too rough for our wheels, and the roads in progress are good indeed. I am sure you have gone through the instructions of her Majesty.

Chief: (Mutters to himself) He talks under his nose like a rat stealing from a pot. What a tone of deceit. He has a white face with dark heart.

Egbaokpe 11: (Looks with consternation) And why should I adhere to the rules and regulations of your ruler?

Norbert Johnson: Do not forget you rule under the British indirect government and you shall work to make Ovokpe kingship a democratic and constitutional monarchy. All people and territories of the land must be bound to the laws of the Queen. Here is the scroll for you to sign into law in respect to the Ovokpe tradition and constitutions, which shall enable democratic processes, take full course in guiding the kingdom.

Otota: (Collects the paper. He and Odogun council goes through the detail.)

Norbert Johnson: Her Majesty, the Queen of Great Britain and Ireland, Empress of India, humbly requests, that all ministers of the Christian religion shall have permit to reside and exercise their calling within territories of the land. All forms of religious worship and religious ordinances will hold within the territories. You shall submit disputes between traditional worshippers and the missionaries, between chiefs and neighbouring tribes, which Ovokpe leadership cannot settle amicably. Her Majesty will exercise jurisdiction in territories for arbitration and decision, or for arrangement.

Egbaokpe 11:   We will adhere to your queen's request, on the condition that this foreign god and missionaries will not attempt to contest superiority over the Ovokpe traditional religious system. For centuries, we have held our worship sacred. We will not entertain any form of disregard to our societal norms and values. My people will have it no other way. Osolobrughwẹ is supreme to us. Let those who want to willingly taste of your gospels go in peace. (The atmosphere is resolute. Light Fades.)

ACT THREE

SCENE ONE

(There is a dance performance festival in the palace. When Irhimvweke comes on stage with her ema ensemble, her supporters begin to eulogize her.)

Supporters: Ekpẹkpẹrẹ (short, but strong)

Irhimvweke: Ugbẹn oghwẹ ọbra (fat thigh of salmon fish)

Supporters: Agbin (the unshakeable).

Irhimvweke: Mia sa ne (I am now coming.)

Supporters: Olorogun (great warrior)

Irhimvweke: Mẹmẹ ọ (I am she)

(The Vweke woman begins to dance with ema music-a mixture of Edo and Ovokpe language. To display her wealth, she changes successively into three expensive dresses and receives rousing ovation and admiration from the audience. As she performs, five children make appearance on stage.)

Vweke Supporters: (Whispers) These well-dressed mixed colour children are born of her wombs with a white man.

Irhimvweke: (Shocked) Who brought them here.

(Some supporters quickly take her and the

children away.)

Citizens:	(They joyfully hail the dancer.) Irhimvweke! Agbin!

Vweke Supporters: They rejoice with Irhimvweke unashamedly. They can hardly sing songs completely in their language.

Citizens: (Sad and shamefaced) This mockery is too much with us.

Vweke Supporters: Go, people of Ovokpe compose songs fully in your indigenous language. Stop borrowing dialects from various tribes to flesh up your skeletal lyrics.

Citizens: (Looks unhappy) This is a great challenge for the people of Ovokpe.

(Light fades and later shines on the council of chiefs.)

Otota: Evgbikume Avzano of Uvghwoton and Evmemo Hemivnagi of Uvgolo, we will not laud your praise names for nothing. Some people of Vweke served us a very bitter pill today. It is too difficult to swallow. We charge both of you with the responsibility to compose new songs in Ovokpe. (They bow and exit.)

Egbaokpe 11:   They mock us. (Sighs) For how long?

Otota: Over the years, the staff of Egbaokpe 1 has grown into a gigantic tree. It has become a sacred grove. I believe it watches us through its branches. Those leaves gather harsh winds and blow it all over the land.

Egbaokpe 11:   Inform the chief priest. We will offer sacrifices to appease the spirit of the late Orodje.

                  (Light fades on them as they proceed to a sacred grove.)

ACT THREE

SCENE TWO

Chorus: Egbaokpe 11 goes home

There are always rifts

When it comes to choosing a king

The curse of Ovokpe not having a king

Is not a pleasant tradition

This consistent interregnum is a plague.

It is Oreovokpe's wish

This holocaust of epileptic kingship will cease

Ovokpe offers more sacrifices to Egbaokpe 1

To free them of this languishing curse

(The elders of Odogun Council are in a meeting to decide which candidates from Olocho ruling house will be crowned Orodje.)

Elder 1:   Prince Wede Otikpe of Olocho ruling house cannot be king.

Elder 2:   Why should we reject his nomination?

Elder 3:   Have you forgotten that his mother is a native of Isoken? Instead, let his cousin, Prince Ogbeke Etie take his place. Or do you want the people of Isoken to come out of the water and take possession of our land through their daughter's son?

Prince Ogbeke: Forgive me, elders of Udogun Council. I cannot honour this nomination because there is a split vote in my family of Etie.

Odogun Council: In that case, you leave the council a choice to appoint Prince Ekeleme Ovokpere of Olocho ruling house as king. (Drums)

Chorus: *His Royal Majesty Olocho I*

Businesses flourish in his reign

He brings tremendous peace

And stability to Ovokpe and their neighbours

He reigns successfully in

The modern life of Oreovokpe

And instills relative peace,

During military rule,

Ovokpe monarchy remains a constitutional institution

His Royal Majesty Olocho I goes home

Kings and chiefs from great kingdoms

OOEE FOUR RULING HOUSES

Military and political sphere

Pays their last respects

ACT THREE

SCENE THREE

(Warlike drums) There is tension in Oreovokpe.

Two contestants tie a vote

On who is to become king?

A descent of Okodide ruling house

Won the favour of the gods

But a squabble

An internal squabble stops

His coronation for many years

At long last he is crowned Orodje of Ovokpe

Mudiaga Fejiro becomes Okodide the first

The people pray this will be

The last of Ovokpe kingship interregnum

(Drums)

(The Palace of Orodje in Ovokpe kingdom. Okodide1 sits with his Council elders in a meeting. Chiefs are in their complete and full regalia of white long sleeve flowing shirt and white wrapper, red long hat, the appropriate traditional chieftaincy beads on the neck, and a pair of white shoes to match.)

Otota:	(Bows) Your majesty, it is time to offer libation to the sacred grove.
Chief:	Yes, it is time. And we hope it will be the last time.
Olorogun:	Your highness, I have just received a call. They want to bury the Okaka of Isoken in Usapele.
Okodide1:	What madness is this? I have decreed, non-indigenes will not lay to final rest in Usapele. I see. They want to test my wrath. Olorogun.
Olorogun:	(Kneels) Your highness.
Okodide:	You know what to do. Send your army, and take back his corpse to Isoken. His soul cannot rest in any Ovokpe.
Olorogun:	(Sheaths his sword. Bows and exits.)
Okodide 1:	(Calms) Let the procession to the sacred grove begin. Prepare the purple candle to repel. We will take our verses from the book of Psalms. (Two priests lead the Orodje out of the palace. Light fades. When it later comes up, there is jubilation on the stage. Drums beat while the entire citizens gather.)
Otota:	People of Ovokpe, our distinguished guests from all around the world, it is a great pleasure

to welcome you all to the birthday ceremony of our Orodje. His Royal Majesty, Okodide 1.

Guests: (Gives the Orodje standing ovation.)

Okodide1:   (The people's claps become faint.) I thank God for having made me a king. He sustains me and that is the major thing about the celebration. The celebration is not just to dance. It is about thanking God. (The entire people applaud. The people roll out drums on stage to dance and celebrate the anniversary of their king. The sounds of abo, feet stamping horrendously echo. Light brightens, showing the king and his chiefs happy with the performances. As the celebration rises to a great momentum, lights fade to a total black out.)

ENGLISH TRANSLATIONS

FIRST OVOKPE CHORUS: ACT ONE-SCENE TWO

Yeah, one requires good luck to become reputable,

Public,

Do not be envious of one another;

If the goat destroys a plantain sucker,

The sucker surely shall grow to maturity in its presence;

Even when they envy the rafia palm,

The palm continues to yield its wine;

Yeah, you are only licking the dirt on our body.

SECOND OVOKPE CHORUS: ACT TWO-SCENE TWO

Umogun was at home,

And the witches looked for his trouble,

Umogun, if I possess the witchery power,

Kill me,

But if I do not have it,

Then leave me alone,

Yes, we, members say so,

Death that people run away from,

You are looking for death yourselves,

And when the death comes,

 To whom would you cry?

The evil the hand causes,

Is what the head follows [pays for].

It has begun,

Grandmother, if we say this,

You (plural) might call it guile (Repeat).